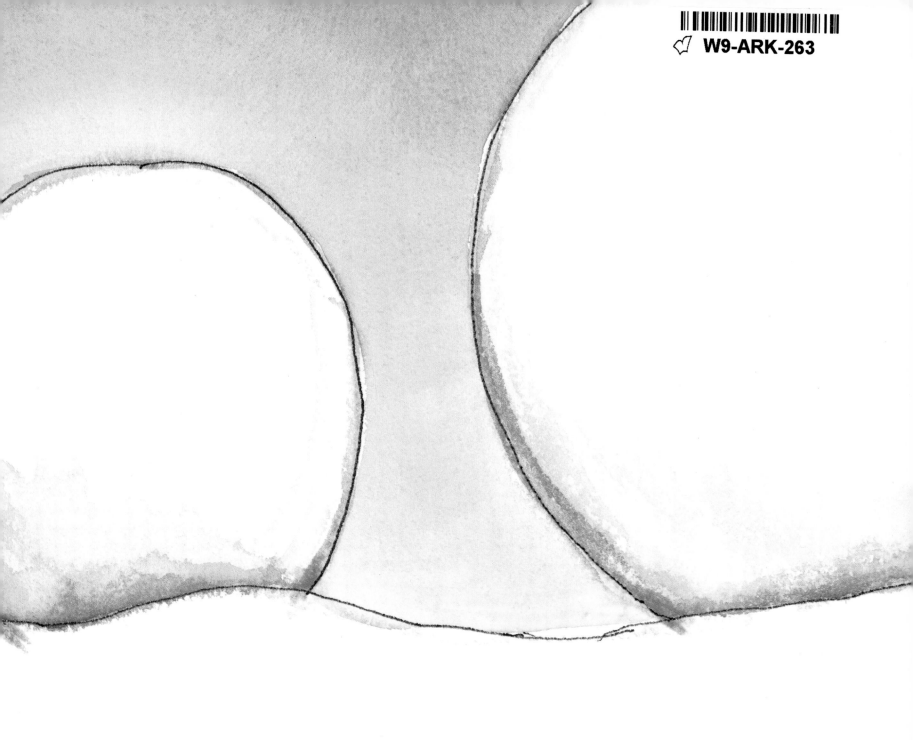

Emmett's
Snowball

By Ned Miller

Pictures by Susan Guevara

Henry Holt and Company • *New York*

Published by Henry Holt and Company, Inc.,
115 West 18th Street, New York, New York 10011.
Published in Canada by Fitzhenry & Whiteside Limited,
195 Allstate Parkway, Markham, Ontario L3R 4T8.

Library of Congress Cataloging-in-Publication Data
Miller, Ned.
  Emmett's snowball / by Ned Miller ; pictures by Susan Guevara.
  Summary: Emmett rolls a snowball in his yard and, with the help
of several friends, soon makes it large enough to be featured
prominently in the town square.
  ISBN 0-8050-1394-6
  [1. Snow—Fiction.] I. Guevara, Susan, ill. II. Title.
PZ7.M63148Em   1990
[E]—dc20   89-77787

Henry Holt books are available at special discounts
for bulk purchases for sales promotions, premiums,
fund-raising, or educational use. Special editions
or book excerpts can also be created to specification.

    For details contact:

    Special Sales Director
    Henry Holt and Company Inc.
    115 West 18th Street
    New York, New York, 10011

First Edition
Printed in the United States of America
10 9 8 7 6 5 4 3 2 1

For my parents
   N.M.

For Blair, as I knew him in Connecticut
                              S.G.

One cold winter morning Emmett woke up early.
He didn't get out of bed. He just waited and listened.
    I hope the whistle blows today, Emmett said to himself.
When the town whistle blew, that meant snow.
On snowy days there was no school.

The whistle blew! Emmett popped out of bed.
He got dressed in a hurry and ran outside.

The ground was white. The trees were white. The house was even whiter than before. The snow was almost a foot deep!

But it was still very early. There was no one for Emmett to play with.

Emmett made a snowball in his hands.

He started to roll it around the yard.

Soon the snowball was half as tall as Emmett. But it was getting heavy and hard to push. And almost all the snow in Emmett's yard was used up.

Emmett's best friend, Sarah, came out of
the house next door. "Hey," Sarah said.
"Pretty big snowball."

"Come over and help me push it,"
Emmett said.

Emmett and Sarah pushed the snowball
through Sarah's front gate and into Sarah's
yard.

Soon the snowball was taller than
Emmett. It was almost as tall as Sarah!

"We could use more help," Sarah said.

Just then Sarah's older brother, Craig, came out. "Big snowball," Craig said.

"We want to make it bigger," said Emmett, "but it's too heavy to move."

"It's not too heavy for *me*," Craig said. Craig was always bragging.

Emmett, Sarah, and Craig rolled the snowball out front again. It was almost too wide for the big double gate.

"Let's take it to the park," Craig said. "We can get it *really* big there!"

By the time they got to the park, the snowball was as tall as Craig.

They came to the top of a long hill. "Let's roll the snowball down the hill," said Emmett.

"Great idea!" said Craig.

But Sarah looked worried. "What if it rolls *too far*?"

Craig pointed. "See that big, strong wooden fence? That will stop the snowball for sure."

"Yeah," said Emmett. "Let's roll it!"

Sarah still looked worried. But she got behind the snowball with Emmett and Craig. They gave a push. The snowball wouldn't budge!

"We need more help," Emmett said.

"Here comes somebody," said Sarah. A tall boy in a bright green jacket was coming across the park.

"He won't help us," Craig said. "That's Danny Campbell. He's in the eighth grade. He hates little kids."

Danny Campbell walked up and put his hand on the snowball. He was trying to act cool, but Emmett could tell he was interested. "Pretty big snowball," Danny Campbell said.

"Want to help us roll it down the hill?" Emmett asked.

Danny Campbell thought about it awhile. Then he said, "Okay!"

They all got behind the snowball and pushed.

Emmett felt his feet slipping.

Sarah, Craig, and Danny Campbell all fell down at the same time. Right on top of Emmett.

The snowball rolled away, down the hill, moving faster and faster.

The snowball rolled right over the big, strong wooden fence! It kept going, straight for the back of Mr. Wetzel's candy store!

"No, no!" Emmett said. "Not the candy store!"

Mr. Wetzel looked out his back window. His round face turned white. His eyes opened wide. The snowball was rolling right at him.

He'll never let me buy M&Ms again, Emmett thought. No more Gummi Bears! No more Bonomo's Turkish Taffy!

There was a loud noise. It sounded something like *"Foomp!"*

The snowball stopped. Everything was quiet.

After a moment Mr. Wetzel came running up the hill. His face wasn't white anymore. It looked like a big, round, red M&M.

Craig and Danny Campbell turned and ran.

"Let's go," Sarah said to Emmett. But Emmett was too scared to move.

When Mr. Wetzel got closer, he started yelling. He yelled and yelled. Sarah put her hands over her ears.

"Your snowball is blocking my back door!" Mr. Wetzel yelled. "How am I supposed to take out the garbage?"

"We could move it," Emmett said.

Mr. Wetzel stopped yelling. "What did you say?" he asked.

"We could move the snowball," Emmett said.

Mr. Wetzel looked back down the hill. After a moment he said, "I suppose we *could* move it, if we had help."

Mr. Wetzel rounded up some people from the other stores on Main Street. They all got behind the snowball and pushed. Emmett and Sarah pushed too. Even Craig and Danny Campbell came back. They rolled the snowball away from Mr. Wetzel's door.

Mr. Wetzel stopped traffic while they rolled it across Main Street.

When they got to the town square, they decided to roll the snowball around a little more. By the time they stopped, it was twice as tall as the statue of President Millard Fillmore.

"It's a world record for sure," said Craig.

While they were all admiring the snowball, a man from the town newspaper came by.

He asked Emmett and Sarah to stand in front of the snowball. Then he took their picture. But Danny Campbell stuck his hand in front of Emmett's face at the last second. The picture was in the paper the next day.

After that, the snowball was famous. People came from all the nearby towns to look at it. Mr. Wetzel sold them lots of candy.

The town even put up lights so everybody could see the snowball at night.

BIGGEST SNOWBALL IN HISTORY!!!

Emmett Smith and Sarah Thomas are responsible for creating the biggest snowball this county has ever seen. Some people in this town feel it is the biggest snowball that has ever been made. On the morning of Nov. 4th the first snow of the season fell

Then people started to forget
about the snowball.
   Soon the weather got warm.
   The snowball began to melt.
   Before long it was down to
President Millard Fillmore's eyebrows.
   Then President Millard Fillmore's
knees.
   Then the platform that President
Millard Fillmore was standing on.

Finally the snowball
was so small that Emmett
could scoop it up
in his hands.

MILLARD F
13ᵗʰ PRESIDE
THE UNITED

Emmett took the snowball home
and put it in the freezer.
"Next time," he said, "I'll make it
even bigger."

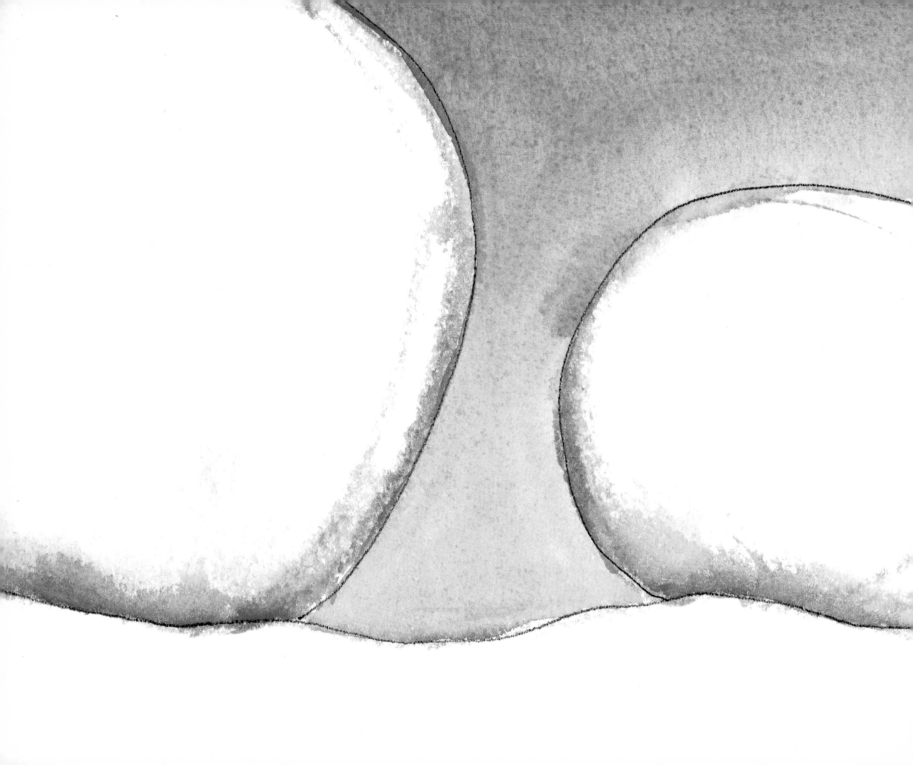